Birds and Their Nests

Carmel Reilly

Contents

Where Birds Make Their Nests

Nests are places where birds lay their eggs.
Birds look after their babies in nests.

Birds make nests in trees,
on the ground or in **burrows**.

They lay their eggs on **cliffs**,
in buildings or in bird boxes.

Nests can be found in lots of places!

Nests in Trees

Lots of birds make their nests in trees.

They build their nests from things
they find around the trees.

These birds make a home in the treetops.
They are safe above the ground,
where other animals cannot find them.

Nests on the Ground

Birds can make their nests
in lots of places on the ground.

There are birds that build nests in the grass.

There are others that hide their nests
under plants or small trees.

Some birds lay eggs in little holes they make in the ground.

Other birds lay eggs on top of rocks.

Nests in Burrows

There are birds that make their nests in burrows.

Some of these birds
dig the burrows themselves.
Others find old burrows
that they can move into.

Burrows are good places for birds to keep their eggs safe and warm.

Nests on Cliffs

Lots of birds build nests on cliffs near the sea.

Cliffs are great places for nests. They are a long way above the sea and safe from other animals.

Cliffs are near to food, too.
Birds can quickly fly down to catch fish
for themselves and their babies.

Nests in Buildings

Sometimes, birds make nests in buildings. A building can be a warm, dry and safe place to live.

This bird has made its nest inside a shed.

Some birds make their nests
on the sides of houses and sheds.

Other birds build their nests
on top of big city buildings.

These birds have built a nest high up on a city building.

Nests in Bird Boxes

Some people put bird boxes in their gardens.
They want to give the birds
a safe place to make their nests.

Nests can be found in trees,
on the ground or in burrows.
They can be in gardens,
on city buildings or by the sea.

Birds make nests in lots of places!

Glossary

burrows holes in the ground dug by small animals

cliffs steep, rocky land by the sea